All the Hope We Carry

Also by Susan Marshall

Fiction

The Makeshift Girl series:

Makeshift Girl: The Secret Heritage Trail

Poetry

Yesterday's Wisdom

Trekking an Age of Light

Evergold Dream

Plays

The Theatre Playscapes series:

Fleur of Yesterday

Single, Full-length Plays:

Indigo's Haven

Broken World

Essays & Articles

Theatre Playscapes: A New Theatrical Style

THEATRE PLAYSCAPES SERIES

All the Hope We Carry

SUSAN MARSHALL

Published in Australia in 2023 by
Story Playscapes
Victoria, Australia
ABN 62197863313

publications@storyplayscapes.com
www.storyplayscapes.com

 A catalogue record for this book is available from the National Library of Australia

NATIONAL LIBRARY OF AUSTRALIA

Title:	All the Hope We Carry
Series:	Theatre Playscapes Series: No.2
Author:	Susan Marshall
ISBN:	9780645404135
Subjects:	Young Adult Fiction / Performing Arts / Theatre & Musicals
	Young Adult Fiction / Fantasy / Contemporary
	Young Adult Fiction / War & Military
Age:	15+

Produced by Story Playscapes
Written by Susan Marshall
Book design, photography and digital art by Ryan Marshall
All images Copyright © Story Playscapes

In her creation of *All the Hope We Carry,* the author, Susan Marshall has revised, adapted and updated her original play, *Indigo's Haven* in order to meet the requirements of her new Theatre Playscapes theatrical style. The original publication of *Indigo's Haven* is written by Susan Marshall and published by RMDesigned in 2016. Copyright © Susan Marshall, 2016.

Dedicated to my Nanna and Nonno Debrincat.
A tribute to the war survivor.

Contents

	8	Theatre Playscapes of Hope
	19	Performance Rights
	20	Characters
	21	Setting
Act 1	22	Act 1, Scene 1
	27	Act 1, Scene 2
	32	Act 1, Scene 3
	35	Act 1, Scene 4
	41	Act 1, Scene 5
	45	Act 1, Scene 6
	48	Act 1, Scene 7
	51	Act 1, Scene 8
	54	Act 1, Scene 9
	56	Act 1, Scene 10
	58	Act 1, Scene 11
	65	Act 1, Scene 12
	68	Act 1, Scene 13
Act 2	70	Act 2, Scene 1
	75	Act 2, Scene 2
	77	Act 2, Scene 3
	83	Act 2, Scene 4
	85	Act 2, Scene 5
	88	Act 2, Scene 6
	92	Act 2, Scene 7
	95	Act 2, Scene 8
	98	Act 2, Scene 9
	102	About the Author
	105	Acknowledgements
	106	About the Book Designer
	106	About Story Playscapes

In her article: *Theatre Playscapes of Hope,* award-winning Susan Marshall shares how her own family history of survival of World War II in Gozo has led to her focus on the heartfelt significance of hope for the war survivor. Using her new Theatre Playscapes style, she has developed her play: *All the Hope We Carry* for young adults.

Theatre Playscapes of Hope
by Susan Marshall

When developing our autonomy throughout our lives, we can learn how to sit with who we are and be at ease. The way we carry ourselves, holistically, in our own lifeworlds is truly special and represents our own uniqueness. I refer to a quote by Amy Cuddy, a social psychologist, in her book: *Presence: Bringing Your Boldest Self to Your Biggest Challenges:*

> "Presence emerges when we feel personally powerful, which allows us to be acutely attuned to our most sincere selves. In this psychological state, we are able to maintain presence even in the very stressful situations that typically makes us feel distracted and powerless."[1]

Above, Amy Curry refers to the importance of becoming aware of our own personal presence. By learning to become comfortable with who we are and how we carry ourselves, we can begin to share parts of our lives with others.

There are times in our lives, where our lifeworlds are grossly impacted by events that are not in our control. The turmoil and uncertainty of such events challenge us to rediscover who we are, in order to adapt or to even survive them.

I have fond memories of my late Nanna, whose presence and wisdom was strong, even in the quieter moments. At her kitchen table, I would sit, admiring her beautiful lace table cloth, which travelled with her from her native homeland in Gozo. I would find comfort in her being there, next to me, eating the warm chicken soup she made and having her comforting hand hold mine.

One day, in my senior years of high school, I had the privilege of interviewing my Nanna as a person who had significant influence in my life. My mother (Nanna's daughter), sat with us, so as to share in the experience. It was during this time that my Nanna was relieved to share, for the first time, her experiences of surviving World War II in Gozo. She expressed her desire to make others aware that as a war survivor, quite a distance away from Valletta, Malta, she had no idea of why the war was occurring. No news or information came to her or others. She and her family were left to cope and survive all they could in their home.

The dark sense of "the other," who were unrelenting with their fury, traumatised my Nanna and her family.

With wisdom, my Nanna also shared with me the significance of the hope that she carried and tried her best, as a young mother, to share with her children. In such traumatic times, hope and faith were two essential values that kept her going.

All the Hope We Carry is a tribute to the war survivor, who, faced with the traumas and turbulence of war, must find a way to carry themself and to survive. It is a fictional play inspired by my Nanna and Nonno's experiences during World War II in Gozo, an island in the Maltese archipelago.

Using the Theatre Playscapes style, I have focused on the convention: **spirit of character** in order to develop Doris, Samuel and Claire, as war survivors. They are a family, yet each have their own unique presence, which is demonstrated through the ways they carry themselves and share their skills with others in their lifeworlds.

In the play, I decided to assist Doris, Samuel and Claire's spirits to grow and transcend beyond their lifeworlds. To achieve this, I engaged in extensive research of the significant role that Malta had as a country, during World War II. As Colonel Edward C. Short states in his article: *Malta: Strategic Impact During World War II*:

> "No discussion of World War II is complete without an examination of the role that the tiny island of Malta played in the conflict. Primarily because of its location and proximity to supply lines, Malta became the most important base of operation in the entire Mediterranean.

> "World leaders, historians and strategists have argued from the time of World War II until the present that the entire outcome of the war rested directly on the fate of the tiny island. F.M. Hinsley, historian and military strategist, contended that the inability of the Axis Powers to capture the island was probably the single most important factor in the overall failure of the Axis effort, especially in North Africa and the Mediterranean."[2]

Malta was a desired island to control and faced much trauma and hardship. This left me with the challenge of bringing Malta at war to life, in a fictional manner, in a way that was suitable for a young adult readership.

I was inspired by Gozo to create the fictional island of Maren that the Attard family reside in. Respecting my Nanna's hope to share the civilian's non-understanding of reasons for war, I have focused on heightening the senses of hope that drive the characters. Such focus enabled me to unravel their adaptations, decisions and proceeding spiritual growth.

There is a moment in the play when young Claire speaks about her island:

CLAIRE
"The familiar tune returns,
its drifting quality heightened in pitch,
like the sound of a bird,
free flying through the soft breeze.

"I allow myself to believe
that I may just be that bird,
taking a small adventure
across my tiny island.

"I could have wings that soar,
high above the red stained streets
into a much calmer, brighter sky.

"I am on the cool sand now,
kicking my heavy shoes off
and letting my feet sink deeply
into the precious, soft granules.

"The shore of Maren, my island home,
once a place of peace and community.
Its sand now dug frantically with trenches,
to protect our army from *them*.

"A fighter jet burns through the sky,
startling me with its loud roar.
Jumping into one of the trenches,
I stand wobbly on two feet,
clutching at whatever earth will hold me up.

"The sand tears away from its shelter,
forming large clumps in my hands.
An earth that has given up resisting,
a warning of the deterioration of Maren.

"So vulnerable we are, on this island,
a short boat ride away from the city of Amarinda.
Yet so unaware, are we all, of why
we suffer such dangerous attacks."[3]

Using the conventions: **immersive language** and **transformation of moment,**
I work to unravel Claire's saturation in her lifeworld: her resulting hopes to
fly up high, like a bird (heightened kinetic energy), away from the 'red stained
streets' into a calmer sky. As the moment transforms, she places her feet onto
the cool sand and is faced with the confrontation of trench dug sand, when
once before it was a place of peace and community. Transforming moment
once more, she is forced to hide in one of the trenches in order to protect
herself from a fighter jet that is scouting the island from above. In these
moments, Claire is adapting to the uncertain and dangerous world - she is
learning how to carry herself within it - her spirit is growing.

Doris, Claire's mother, has remained mostly confined to her home in Maren.
She wishes to protect her children. She also hopes to find her son, Samuel,
who has disappeared. I worked to create **heightened energy** in the home,

via references to the desire for light. Whether it is the radiant energy of sunlight or moonlight filtering through the window or the thermal heat of a kerosene lamp or matchsticks, light is an essential, symbolic representation of hope. It helps to fuel the development of character presence and spirit.

To further develop Doris' hopes and the journeys of her spirit of character, I have referred to a key essential belief during World War II for the people of Malta. It is faith, predominately reflected through the Catholic religion. Il-Bambina, or the feast of Our Lady's birth (Victory Day), is a significant spiritual time for Maltese people nationally, as it commemorates the end of two sieges that existed in Malta:

> "This feast is very dear to us and our history, as it reminds us of our roots," the Archbishop said. "When Maltese were trying to seize their destiny in their own hands, they always thought of this day as the one which made them who they are."[4]

Throughout the play, Doris and her family's belief in Lady Solary's ability to carry the light of hope and mercy during war, was inspired by Il-Bambina. To carry hope of her presence, is to carry hope in faith and life, as is journeyed throughout the play.

In a moment of heightened energy, Doris reveals her need for the light of Lady Solary. She plays with her shadow and its patterns, to show how she carries herself.

DORIS

"A walking shadow I have become,
my soul's pockets empty of life.

"I see my shadow now,
flittering closely behind me,
determined to follow my trails
into the encroaching darkness.

"My feet, when lifted, leave patterns
of life once walked upon Maren's grounds.
Patterns I long to retrace and rediscover,
in the beauty of Lady Solary's light.

"I once thrived in her light,
my body taller and carrying me confidently.
A wife, I was, to my loving husband, Ray.
A home we made with our beautiful children.

"Honest lives we lived,
in the security of Maren's embrace.

"Yet now, Maren has changed.

"Foreign are my footprints now,
striking so cautiously across the ground.

12

"I am without husband,
my soul yearning to save my daughter from the war.

"Be the hope you wish to see.

"I remember those words,
once shared with me by Ray,
as the darkness of the war crept in on us.

"Watch my shadow, I can now,
as it twirls independently,
away from my body.

"Dancing, my shadow is now,
along with yours, Ray.
Embracing and twirling they are,
like we used to at dusk."[5]

Such interactions with Doris' shadow, can also be achieved by the convention: **animated lifeworld.** This enables the contemporary, war landscape to be heightened, in order to reveal Doris' subconscious desires and memories through shadow play.

Another way that Doris carries hope, is via her role as a hospitaller woman. She is skilled in providing medical care to the injured or sick and so nurses four civilians, who have escaped the hostilities of Amarinda, the closest island. References to the civilians' experiences in Amarinda are based on research I have undertaken on Valletta and Senglea during World War II. It includes the attack of the parish (Senglea) and also the bombing of a navy ship (Valletta).

The roles of women in hospitaller services play a significant, historical part of Maltese culture, particularly under the Sovereign Order of Malta, which states in their article: *Nuns of the Order of Malta*:

"Scholars date the origin of the female branch to the Order's foundation in Jerusalem in the 11th century and to the first consecrated nuns of the Hospital of St Mary Magdalena. The nuns were needed in the hospitals to tend the female pilgrims and patients and were led by the Servant of God Agnese of Alix. Over time they increased in number and organisation; they continued to embrace the ideal and charisma of the Order of St. John and to spread out across most of Europe to Italy, Spain, Portugal, Great Britain, France, Denmark, Holland and Rhodes [...]

"The Monastery of St Ursula in Valletta, Malta was founded by Grand Master Verdalle in 1582, in the Grand Master's Palace in Birgu, which had been left vacant since the Order established itself in Valletta. In 1595 the monastery was transferred to Valletta. The nuns were equal in rank to the chaplain brothers of the Order, observed the rules of the cloister, and were under the Grandmaster's jurisdiction. In their religious solemn profession the nuns vow to observe the Rule of the Order of St. John of Jerusalem, following the practice established at their foundation, which continues uninterrupted up to the present day."[6]

Doris herself, attempts to hold onto the light that Lady Solary provides her with spiritually. As a hospitaller woman, caring for others and by also watching the deterioration of the world around her, she is worn out and desperate for a solution to save her own family.

DORIS

"It's alright Claire, we all need light.
Lady Solary's presence is weak during
these troubled times.

"Let me light the lamp."[7]

Throughout the play, Doris undertakes a spiritual journey that involves her recognising the positive impacts and presence of hope in lifeworlds. By learning to see what is before her, in its human and spiritual presence, she may be able to have her hopes fulfilled.

Doris is completely unaware that transcending beyond her space, is a new lifeworld. Her son, Samuel, drawn into a moment of **situational pull**, has entered the world of a paper playscape:

SAMUEL

"This room appears small and dark now.
Yet, facing this paper, I feel big.

"I can feel a strong light glowing
inside my excited, pounding heart.

"Hope.

"Is that what I reach for now?

"Let me take that step.

"The paper feels slippery beneath my feet.

"Am I growing?
Or is the world disappearing?

"Gone is the living room I once stood in.
Confined it was, locking my soul away.

"I can take larger, lighter steps now
and inhale grateful gulps of much clearer air.

"I am awash with a sea of gratitude,
that fills every crevice of my body.
I feel as though I am floating freely
out across a wide, calm ocean.

"So tired I am, feeling fatigue in every muscle.
For so long I have stayed awake ...

"I am the protector of my mother and sister."[8]

The paper playscape is a world that continues to flourish around Samuel and works to support his healing and spiritual growth. It is a world that his sister Claire creates, with her exceptional drawing skills on paper. A world that she hopes will heal and protect the war survivors of her world.

The paper playscape unravels its identity to be a fantastical picture grassland, which was inspired by much research into the physiography of both Gozo and Ghar Dalam in Malta.

John J. Borg, the Curator at the Natural History Unit of Heritage Malta, details in his publication: *Ghar Dalam: Workbook*:

> "The Maltese Islands started to form around 35 million years ago, when sediments and dead marine organisms (plants and animals) were deposited onto a shallow seabed close to a large land mass. By time these sediments hardened and solidified. The deposition of material kept going on for some 30 million years."[9]

As a result of the above processes, different rock layers were formed on the islands. The first layer consists of lower coraline limestone, which is made up of a combination of algae from the sea, along with small animals found in rocks, such as urchins and oysters. The second rock layer is Globigerina limestone (made from the calcium in the tiny snail's shell). Blue clay sits on top of this limestone. Adorning some areas of Malta, is a layer of green sand, typically discovered in Gozo. Finally, the top rock layer is upper coraline limestone, which is not evident on the south side of the Maltese islands.[10]

The physiography of Malta, as explained above, was essential in my development of the worlds in this play. For example, the creation of a limestone cave was vital to forming a place of survival for the people who inhabited the picture grassland.

John Borg's description of the development of Ghar Dalam was useful in providing a sense of life lived to the picture grassland:

> "The overflowing river gradually 'ate' its way deeper and deeper into the limestone until it reached the tunnel's roof and breached it. This formation of the cave happened in the early periods of the Ice Age, but the collapse of the cave's roof happened when herds of hippopotami and elephants roamed the Maltese countryside. The opening of the tunnel roof acted as a swallow-hole. Soil, pebbles, stones, carcasses of dead animals, dismembered skeletal parts and other debris dragged by the river were sucked into the tunnel and deposited within."[11]

In this play, references to bones, injury and remnants of life are motifs of lives lived and lost during the war. At home in Maren, Claire is afraid of the broken bodies that she has witnessed in war and also believes are present in her own home. As she draws the picture grassland, bones and injury become part of the fantastical world. They are first noticed by Samuel on its grassland and much later, in a cave.

The cave itself, is a place of refuge in the picture grassland. John J Borg in his publication: *Ghar Dalam: a shelter for WWII refugees and military fuel supplies*, refers to the significance of the cave during World War II:

> "A less known aspect of the history of Ghar Dalam is connected with the outbreak of the Second World War. The constant bombing that the Maltese Islands endured in the war forced many Maltese to abandon their homes and seek shelter away from the prime danger zones. On 11 June 1940, a day after Italy declared war on Britain and France, a series of air raids was carried out on these islands. The prime targets were the harbour areas and the airfields. Following one of these early raids along the southern coast of Malta, particularly on Mal Far airfield and the Royal Navy Air Station at Kalafrana, the handful of residents at Mal Far and Benghisa packed a few belongings and headed off in search of a safe shelter away from the bombed areas. A few kilometres away, safely tucked along the side of a narrow valley, lay a natural shelter that would serve their purpose [....] and they flocked inside this dark shelter."[12]

Using the convention: situational pull, I have created a moment where Samuel is made to face a situation concerning war refugees in a cave. It is a moment of spiritual growth for Samuel, where he becomes aware of his instinctive need to care for the lives of others.

To develop the remaining picture grassland, I researched the physiography and land use of the island of Gozo during World War II. Colonel Edward C. Short explains this landscape and its resources further:

> "Malta is made of limestone rock and is poor in most resources. There are no lakes, rivers and only a few trees. Although the soil is fertile, it is very, very scarce [...]

> "Agriculture was never a major economic benefit to the island. The Maltese farmed only as it met their immediate needs. Author Jan Hay who was stationed on the island both before and during the Second World War, recalled that the inhabitants of Malta depended for their existence upon a livelihood wrung from the ocean or from a quarter acre tomato and lettuce patch [...]"[13]

The picture grassland details a mixture of the world of Maren that Claire remembers, along with new innovations that she wishes existed, such as more grassland, pine trees, herbs, a waterfall etc. to ensure healing and livability. Claire also develops Yarrow, a cat-like creature who helps to care for the world.

The picture grassland can involve much play with its animated lifeworlds. While its continuous growth and fantasy are detailed throughout the play, I have left it up to young performers to decide which parts of this lifeworld they wish to animate via visual stagecraft (e.g. puppetry) or performance (e.g. acrobatics) techniques. The construction of the animated lifeworld by the performer, should enable them to engage in ideas for what a grassland of hope should highlight through performance - what world impression they wish to share with their audience.

A discussion of this play's creation would not be complete without reference to the significance of the biplanes endearingly called Faith, Hope and Charity by Maltese war survivors. To understand their significance, one must know their backgrounds, as detailed below by the WWII National War Museum (New Orleans) in their article: *Forgotten Fights: Malta's Faith, Hope, and Charity, 1940*.

> "Maynard's mechanics eventually were able to assemble six of the Gladiators, but this only allowed them to put three aircraft in the air at any one time, with the other three being used as backups and for spare parts. Still, the British were desperate to be able to put anything into the air against the Italians—not just to interfere with their bombing raids, but to prove to the people of Malta that somebody was fighting to defend them against enemy bombs [...]

> "Still, the Gladiators gave all they had. As Maltese civilians gathered to watch the air combat in the clear blue Mediterranean skies, they were delighted to see the biplanes swoop fearlessly to engage the Italians. The biplanes were immediately recognizable because of their shape, and soon seemed to take on personalities of their own to those watching from below. Somewhere along the way they acquired the nicknames of Faith, Hope, and Charity.

> "Over the 10 days from June 11-21, 1940, these three Gladiators (really six aircraft used interchangeably) and their dedicated volunteer pilots formed Malta's only defense against enemy bombing raids."[14]

It is these planes: Faith, Hope and Charity, that inspired me to create the Mist in this play.

MIST
"A young girl's stroke has breathed us life
upon this luscious, grassy meadow.
Unbound we float in the aether,
protecting the sanctuary of life below.

"To grow, this world needs nurturing
only Lady Solary's warmth can provide.
Yet light flickers briefly then fades,
like a struck match failing to ignite."[15]

Using the convention of heightened energy, I create the Mist as a living, kinetic motion, that is determined to heal and protect the picture grassland. It is a helper and a saviour in this play.

It has been a heart touching journey writing this play. I hope you enjoy your discoveries!

Susan Marshall
Founder, Australian Author, Theatre Practitioner & Publisher,
Story Playscapes

19 September, 2023

Endnotes:

1   Cuddy, Amy (2015): *Presence: Bringing Your Boldest Self to Your Biggest Challenges* (The Legacy Triilogy). Orion, United Kingdom.

2   Colonel Edward C. Short (Special Forces United States Army), COL (Ret) Brian Moore, USMC (Project Advisor) (2000): *Malta: Strategic Impact During World War II*. U.S. Army War College, Carlisle Barracks, Pennsylvania. Accessed at: https://apps.dtic.mil/sti/pdfs/ADA378250.pdf

3   Marshall, Susan L. (2023): *All the Hope We Carry*. Story Playscapes, Melbourne, Australia, pp.41–42.

4   Times of Malta (2019): *Feast of Maria Bambina given highest ranking in liturgical calendar: Pope Francis makes feast a solemnity following bishops' request*. Accessed at: https://timesofmalta.com/articles/view/feast-of-maria-bambina-given-highest-ranking-in-liturgical-calendar.734026

5   Marshall, Susan L. (2023): *All the Hope We Carry*. Story Playscapes, Melbourne, Australia, p.59.

6   Sovereign Order of Malta (n.d.): *Nuns of the Order of Malta*. Accessed at: https://www.orderofmalta.int/about-the-order-of-malta/nuns-of-the-order/

7   Marshall, Susan L. (2023): *All the Hope We Carry*. Story Playscapes, Melbourne, Australia, p.32.

8   Marshall, Susan L. (2023): *All the Hope We Carry*. Story Playscapes, Melbourne, Australia, pp.23–24.

9   Borg, John J (2007) *Ghar Dalam: A Workbook*. A Visitor Services Division Project, Heritage Malta.

10 Borg, John J (2007) *Ghar Dalam: A Workbook*. A Visitor Services Division Project, Heritage Malta.

11 Borg, John J (2007) *Ghar Dalam: A Workbook*. A Visitor Services Division Project, Heritage Malta.

12 Borg, John J (2006/2007) *Ghar Dalam: a shelter for WWII refugees and military fuel supplies*. Malta Archaeological Review, Issue 8. Accessed at: https://www.um.edu.mt/library/oar/bitstream/123456789/50161/1/Ghar%20Dalam%20a%20shelter%20for%20WWII.pdf

13 Colonel Edward C. Short (Special Forces United States Army), COL (Ret) Brian Moore, USMC (Project Advisor) (2000): *Malta: Strategic Impact During World War II*. U.S. Army War College, Carlisle Barracks, Pennsylvania. Accessed at: https://apps.dtic.mil/sti/pdfs/ADA378250.pdf

14 WWII National War Museum (New Orleans) (2020): *Forgotten Fights: Malta's Faith, Hope, and Charity, 1940*. Accessed at: https://www.nationalww2museum.org/war/articles/british-biplanes-faith-hope-charity-1940

15 Marshall, Susan L. (2023): *All the Hope We Carry*. Story Playscapes, Melbourne, Australia, p.70

Performance Rights

Characters

DORIS ATTARD: a Madam Hospitaller.

CLAIRE ATTARD: Doris' daughter.

SAMUEL ATTARD: Doris' son.

DAHREN   a chorus of Citizens
TRISHA   who transform into
ANTHONY   a chorus of Mist
AYARNA

YARROW: a cat-like creature, a healer.

OFFICIAL VOICE: an army official.

Setting

The heightened energies and actions within the fictional, war-torn island of Maren (in the Attard household, surrounding streets and Food Distribution Office), carry Doris, Claire and the Citizens' spirits of hope.

Claire continually draws a fantastical picture grassland, that is designed to escape the war and to heal the world. Gradual belief in this animated lifeworld and all it offers, also enable Samuel and Doris' spirits to grow.

The play requires minimal set and properties.

Act 1, Scene 1

SAMUEL

It is almost dark now,
nearly time for curfew.
I am sweating profusely.
Lines of fear dash across
every inch of my shaking body.

If I clutch at my heart, it beats fast.

I have not slept properly in weeks.

Hypervigilant, I have been,
dashing across exposed corridors
of what was once my heart's home.
I shield myself in the dim light
and disappear into the shadows.

What have I become?

I live here, yet I am not seen.
The world pulses with bloodshed,
that sends shivers down my spine.

Try, I do, to find places to hide
within the confines of these walls,
away from the rage of metal.

I do not sleep at night.
Instead, I sit with my back to the wall.
I peer outside, like I am now
at the streaks of lamp light,
which cast their knowing rays.

They have witnessed all that is.

Echoes of life call to me,
like sparks of hope in the darkness.
Times of play and freedom …

The trees we would climb,
higher and higher towards the sky,
releasing our dreams towards the heavens.

SAMUEL

I wish I could clutch those hopes now,
secure them tightly in both my fists
and harvest them somehow
in my torn, saddened heart.

I remember wise words once spoken:
if we carry enough hope, we can heal the world.

We are only young, yet old,
aging quickly in a world
that is filled with endless rage.

A world that we wish to calm down.
Talk some sense too.
Ask to start afresh.

Maybe there is a way to end this madness?

I see it there, unrolled and
displayed across the floor.

A simple piece of paper.
Yet it is so much more than that.

There is no one outside.
I am camouflaged in the near darkness.

It is safe to stand.

There are only a few more minutes left
until the air raids shatter my ears.

Enough time for me to venture
towards this special paper ...

A thin slither of moonlight
shines into the living room.
It casts a gorgeous halo of light
around the sheet of paper,
drawing me towards its beauty.

Only a couple more steps now and I am ...

Wow!
The detail is intricate.

This room appears small and dark now.
Yet, facing this paper, I feel big.

SAMUEL

I can feel a strong light glowing
inside my excited, pounding heart.

Hope.

Is that what I reach for now?

Let me take that step.

The paper feels slippery beneath my feet.

Am I growing?
Or is the world disappearing?

Gone is the living room I once stood in.
Confined it was, locking my soul away.

I can take larger, lighter steps now
and inhale grateful gulps of much clearer air.

I am awash with a sea of gratitude,
that fills every crevice of my body.
I feel as though I am floating freely
out across a wide, calm ocean.

So tired I am, feeling fatigue in every muscle.
For so long I have stayed awake ...

I am the protector of my mother and sister.

Now I search for a way for us to escape the
never-ending fury of darkness.

Here is a paper crease,
folded severely by a determined hand.
It is the crossroad that I've been told
to keep an eye out for.

I can do this!

Stepping onto the crease,
I tense my body in anticipation of the worst.

I am rising higher now as the crease grows,
forming into a large, dotted green hill.

It is a grassland, semi arid,
yet green grass shoots up
in tufts here and there.

The air is getting warmer now,
I can feel the sun shining on my skin.

SAMUEL

Lying on my back, I dare myself to surrender
to a moment of pure joy.

Whee!
I am rolling down the hill!
The sheer thrill ...

Flat earth lies beneath me,
semi arid, with more tufts of grass.
Beneath me, strange lines and shapes are sketched.
I trace them with my fingers,
trying to decipher what they are.

On contact, the lines begin to rise,
growing taller and taller
and forming into pine trees,
swaying high in the distance.

The trees are just as I remember.

It will be great to wrap my arms
around their comforting trunks
and climb them, just like I used to.

It was such a long time ago.

Whoa!
What is that sound?

I can feel my body tense again,
this time with deep fear.

In this light, I am exposed.
I could be spotted by *them*.

That scary sound again.
One I know all to well.

Why can't I escape it?

It is the sound of gunfire.
So distant, yet so close.

Silence does not last long here.

I must keep moving.

The sketched land is void of any human life,
except for the broken bones.
Praying I don't tread on them,
I take on a slow jog.

SAMUEL

I pick up my pace,
surprised at my speed.
The wind beats against my face.

More grass ... where did it come from?

Slowing down, I forget the gunfire.
The new grass was not sketched.
Yet it appears here, like magic.

Now the grass is knee high.
Tall enough to hide in.

I drop onto the ground,
rolling onto my stomach,
peering between the blades.

For now I am safe.

Act 1, Scene 2

DORIS

My feet step carefully
along the darkened corridor
of my once peaceful home.

Black, so much black paint
smears itself across our windows.
We block out *them,*
yet we also block out light.

The land of Maren, my island,
calls to me in my fretful sleep.
Like dancing ribbons of light,
it winds its memories around
my starved, yearning torso,
tearing at my aching heart.

I am twirling now,
unravelling a ribbon memory
of light, warm sand
and cresting waves around me.

To feel at breath with my
unique, native land
and to retrace my footprints
across its terrains would be ...
heavenly.

The light of my Lady Solary
is tiny, shining up high,
way beyond my reach.

It once shone so brightly,
it burned like the full sun
in the middle of the day.

Lifted my heart, it did,
made me glow with happiness.
A proud mother, I was,
living life under my Lady's guidance.

DORIS

Now dim light shines through
the gaps in the black paint.
It dapples itself across the floor,
attempting to light up our lives.

The joy has shrunk in my heart.

Spinning quickly, is my body,
hoping to somehow lift itself
away from this very darkness
and drift into desired light.

Yet, the light outside is not the same.
It ticks with madness,
expelled by angry bodies.
Natural light has been
outshone by the fire
of angry, wrathful metal.

So we hide, away from war
and the comforting faces
we once shared our lives with.

What is that?

Someone is knocking
at the front door.

It could be *them*.

I am afraid to open the door.

There is that knocking again.
Persistent, it is.

Stepping heavily, I am now,
my hands shaking with fear.

Voices are calling for me,
I can hear them ...

I had better answer the door.

Who is there?

CITIZENS

We are citizens of Amarinda,
the closest island to Maren.
Blessed Solary, our Lady of Light,
led us through the night to you, Madam Hospitaller.

28

DORIS

What has happened?

CITIZENS

Oh magnificent city!
Victorious against the North,
where is your strength now?
Bombs explode and fires rage,
eating our city alive.

DORIS

How horrific!
Was there no shelter to aid you?

CITIZENS

Our parish was attacked.
Is there no mercy?

Oh Lady Solary, hear our prayers!
Bless the power of your bright light,
lead us to victory once more!

DORIS

Blessed Lady Solary.

CITIZENS

Last evening we saw a ship destroyed,
attacked by a cascade of bombs.
Royal Navy Officers bravely fought back,
unafraid of certain death under fire.

As the ship swayed, trying to gain balance,
our people's bodies flew into the water.
Bless those brave and fearless Officers,
working to save their lives.

Our hearts soared with hope and we prayed,
surely the ship would be saved?
A final set of bombs saw its demise,
burying it deeply within the sea.

DORIS

The night is silent and shields you now,
yet fierceness edges its way closer.
I can see the silver barrels glistening
in the stark, deathly silent moonlight.
Like ears they are, pricked
and listening for the slightest sound.

I see that you are all injured.
Please step inside, away from further danger.

We must stay under the radar,
be as quiet as we can.
We do not want to draw attention to ourselves.
Do you understand?

CITIZENS

Yes Madam, we do.
The streets are very dark,
void of any sounds of merriment.

Rather, they are a rageful playground
for those that do not see reason.

We pray that your home may shield us from harm.

DORIS

We can only hope that Lady Solary will grant us mercy.

CITIZENS

Yes, we fervently pray for her grace to save us.

DORIS

Please, sit here.
Let me tend to your wounds.

There we go.

This may sting a little.
Lift your leg so I can bandage your wound.

You all must be very hungry.
Food is short but I will see what I can find.

CITIZENS

No need Madam.
We bring meats from our cattle,
whom we chose to spare the agonies of war.
We are happy to share for your hospitaller.

DORIS

Thank you. My daughter will be very grateful.

I am happy for you to stay here, under one condition.

CITIZENS

What is that, Madam?

DORIS

That my daughter is never exposed to the
horror outside that front door.
Not even through stories.
Is that clear?

CITIZENS

Very clear Madam.
If there is any such exposure,
it won't be from us.
You have our word.

Bless you hospitaller woman,
for opening up your home to us.
Your charity will not be forgotten.
We are forever in your debt.

Act 1, Scene 3

CLAIRE

Can't sleep.
I see ...
A nightmare!

DORIS

Claire, calm down!

CLAIRE

Broken bodies!

DORIS

Claire, these are -

CLAIRE

Screaming faces,
eyes closed tight.
They need to speak.

Broken bodies!
Mother, please fix the broken bodies!

DORIS

I am fixing their bodies, see Claire?
They're bandaged so they can heal.

CLAIRE

No more darkness.
We need more light!

I need to listen,
just for a moment,
to the tune that breathes life ...

DORIS

It's alright Claire, we all need light.
Lady Solary's presence is weak during
these troubled times.

Let me light the lamp.

It's not dark now, it's light.
The people are moving, see?
They are alive.

CLAIRE

The bodies move in the fractured glow
of protruding, white moonlight.
Bodies of the night, I see,
arriving here from Amarinda.

The mysterious lights they carry,
flickering across their bodies,
reveal their states of impermanency.

Wanderers they are, across the
unpredictable wrath of day and night.
Bearers of battle's anguish, they see
more of the world than we, in these confines.

Unknown to us, are the reasons for such fight,
that strip the souls of man with live fire.

Sitting ducks are we, to war's wrath.

You must keep your eyes open.
It is not safe to sleep.
Not safe ...

CITIZENS

The girl is exhausted.

DORIS

Yes. She finds it hard to sleep.
She is plagued by nightmares of war.

I had no idea she would think you were –

CLAIRE

You must keep ...
Not safe ...

DORIS

The state she's in now, I dare not move her.

CLAIRE

You must keep your eyes open,
don't lose yourself here in Maren.
The dark can coax and hide you,
stripping you of your glowing light
and nurturing the very fears that torment you.

CLAIRE

Where is the paper?

I must draw.

The grassland is very dark now.
Yet a fire is scouting through the air.

Samuel must hide.

Act 1, Scene 4

SAMUEL
The night air is still, embracing me
with its residual heat from the day.
Pulling myself up onto my knees,
I stretch my arms out beside me,
immersing myself in the calmness.

The paper below me is shining
with the iridescent glow of moonlight.
Red tipped are the grass blades in its glow,
as though they have been dipped in fire.

Growing taller are the grass blades,
a cluster of sharp, fiery green,
casting an eerie glow in the moonlight.

As the wind grows stronger,
it bends the grass stems towards me.
Like eyes are their reddened tips,
edging closer towards me,
invading my very space, my being.

The wind shifts, echoing in my ears
with its much stronger gusts.
It rustles the paper beneath my feet,
making me stumble and clutch at
the grass blades to hold myself steady.

I feel the searing, burning of my hands,
caught alight by the red-tipped firc.
Silent I am, mesmerised by the flames
that have now caught me in their trap.

Fire is bad.

Fire takes people away.

Claire's words are accurate.
I am in a burning dream world.
One that I may never leave.
My hands and arms are now alight
and my eyes are stinging with tears.

SAMUEL

What am I doing here?

The wind is blowing fiercely now,
propelling the fire that consumes me.
Yet, my hands and arms are still
unscathed and fully intact.

The paper beneath my feet is tilting,
like a tall, steep hill slope.
I am sliding down it,
the strong breeze whistling in my ears.

Reaching out beside me
are my arms and hands,
alight with the blaze of fire.

Accelerating I am now, at lightning speed
down the paper hill slope.
Blurring past me, is the world,
my feet slipping across every surface.

I have reached maximum speed,
my body feeling as light as air.
Leaving the slope,
my feet rise up into the night aether.

Instinctively, I flap my arms beside me,
streaking fire across the sky
with my red flamed, fluttering wings.

High I am, staring down at
the creased world below me.
A world that I have sworn to protect.

I need to return to the paper ground.

What is that?

A glowing red dart is zapping through the air.
It is metal and bird like, with bright red wings.
Its two eyes are dark and evil,
penetrating my gaze with its glare.

It is a bird fire plane,
tearing unrelentingly through the night.

It is *them.*

My instincts are kicking in.
Flexing my body, I twist, avoiding collision.

SAMUEL

The dart tears passed me,
screaming a strange roaring sound
that blares through the night air.

Turning around, I survey my situation.
In the near distance, many bird fire planes
are ripping through the air towards me.

I am under attack!

Zipping through the air
at lightning speed,
I weave a fiery escape trail
that is a beacon of light for the bird fire planes.

Right behind me they are,
almost upon me,
their rageful tension
propelling through night's darkness.

My heart is pounding rapidly,
almost exploding in my throat.
Yet I ignore it, turning my vision
to the land that breathes below me.

The grass, red tipped and glaring,
almost reaches up towards me,
asking permission to join in.

Rising higher into the sky,
I watch as two bird fire planes collide,
exploding into a fiery mass in the sky.

A mass that rapidly dissipates,
exuding remnants of ash, that float aimlessly,
through the dark air, unable to land.

I have less than one minute before contact.

I know exactly what I need to do now.

Staring at the grass blades again,
I am mesmerised by their fiery, red tips.

Instinctively I stretch my arms out wide,
allowing my wings to expand into the air.

Growing my wings are, larger and larger,
the fire in them alight with my determination.

I can do this!

SAMUEL

In response, the grass blades are shooting up higher,
growing taller and taller, as their red tips
yearn to make contact with my blazing wings.

Holding my stance, floating vertically in the air,
I inhale a deep breath of anticipation
as the grass grows taller and taller.

Only a few more seconds and -

A large shock wave tremors
through my body as the red tips of the grass blades
connect with my spanned wings.

I feel my eyes burning aglow with fire
and a confident, powerful beat in my heart.
We are one, united as a barrier,
defending our world from *them*.

Brighter and stronger is our fiery glow,
almost blinding the night sky with our light.

Shattering into millions of tiny pieces
are the bird fire planes,
floating aimlessly away in the night air.

I exhale a breath of relief.

Placing both feet on the red tips of grass blades,
I begin to descend to the ground.

Reducing in size are the grass blades,
growing smaller and smaller until
they are a mere sketch on the paperscape.

Placing one foot in front of the other,
I balance myself as I hit the paper ground.

I am safe.

Placing my arms by my side,
I watch as my own fire gradually extinguishes.

Flexing my fingers, I check my skin for burns or scars.

There are none.

We have defended the paperscape for now,
yet the *other* may return soon.

I need to find a place to hide.

SAMUEL

Ahead, a dim glow seeps
through a group of pine trees.
It is so far, yet so close.

I can do this.

Slowly, I begin to walk,
pressing my feet into the
small, sharp blades of grass.

Roots of this world, are the grass stems,
sturdy and fiery, holding everything together.

So close is a little further.
The light lures me towards it.

Reaching the pine tree,
I lower myself below branches,
avoiding being spotted in the light.

If *they* saw me, it would all be over.

A closer view of the light source
reveals that it is a pine cone,
hanging precariously from a branch.
Its light is radiant in the dark.

So close is so dangerous.
If I am discovered here ...

Pulling the pine cone,
I pry it free from the branch.

As it falls, I catch it in one hand
and try to conceal its brightness.

It begins to dwindle, fading away,
re-adjusting itself to a dim light.

Can the pine cone read my mind?
It seems to know what to do.

The pine cone is directing its light
to the ground in front of the tree.

My gaze darts downwards
and I discover the tree's message.
There is a large hollow trunk
for me to hide in.

SAMUEL

Flexing my body,
I fit into the hollow.

Another co-incidence?

For now, it's time to rest.

Act 1, Scene 5

CLAIRE

A familiar tune plays,
unwinding like a lullaby,
in my tired, woken mind.

Bending my knees slightly,
I press one hand against
the peeling black paint
of the glass window.

No more darkness.
It is time to let some light in.

Pricking my ears, I listen.
There is not a sound nearby.
Everyone must be asleep.

As the window slowly creaks open,
my gaze dashes over my shoulder.
No-one is here.

I feel a gush of cool, evening air,
caressing my pale, dry cheeks.
It is soothing, luring me outside
into the wide, open night scape.

Crawling through the gap
in the window sill,
I press one foot onto the dirt,
followed by the other.

A small chill reverberates down my spine,
yet I ignore it, staring ahead.
I am outside in the dusk now,
my feet trekking across my native earth.

The familiar tune returns,
its drifting quality heightened in pitch,
like the sound of a bird,
free flying through the soft breeze.

I allow myself to believe
that I may just be that bird,
taking a small adventure
across my tiny island.

CLAIRE

I could have wings that soar,
high above the red stained streets
into a much calmer, brighter sky.

I am on the cool sand now,
kicking my heavy shoes off
and letting my feet sink deeply
into the precious, soft granules.

The shore of Maren, my island home,
once a place of peace and community.
Its sand now dug frantically with trenches,
to protect our army from *them*.

A fighter jet burns through the sky,
startling me with its loud roar.
Jumping into one of the trenches,
I stand wobbly on two feet,
clutching at whatever earth will hold me up.

The sand tears away from its shelter,
forming large clumps in my hands.
An earth that has given up resisting,
a warning of the deterioration of Maren.

So vulnerable we are, on this island,
a short boat ride away from the city of Amarinda.
Yet so unaware, are we all, of why
we suffer such dangerous attacks.

I am knee deep in sea water now,
feeling the energy of the tidal waves
as they roll inwards towards the shore.

A tide that exhales life spent,
across its great, red stained sea.
Its waves' beats are out of sync,
as they crawl slowly towards land.

This sand is the last place I stood with Father,
before he left to work on the railways, far away.

The familiar tune swells in my heart now
and I smile through my falling tears.
It is the melody that my father sang to me,
as he held my small hand firmly in his.

CLAIRE

Stretching my arms into the air,
I close my eyes and feel the power
of the waves of the night.

You can always create the world you hope to see.

My voice bounces across the wide, open air.
It sounds as determined as my father's was,
when he said those words
and smiled through the ache in his heart.

My father had the same gift I do,
an ability to bring a world of detail to life.

If I close my weary eyes,
I can shut the dark out,
just for a single moment
and see the world I hope to see.

Unravel its detail does,
so slowly in the dim light.

It is a fragile dream,
half awake, half asleep.
Sketches of a world I yearn to reach.

Out here though, in this night air,
I feel caressed with a sense of hope.
Maybe it is the sea water, soothing me
as it laps gently against my treading body.

This hand, it is mine,
yet when I pick up a pencil
it has a mind of its own.

It has a story to draw,
beating the breath of life
through its lines and shapes,
across the wide, open paper.

If I just attune myself
to the unravelling melody,
I know I will be able to take that journey
and heal the torn, aching world.

I know that my father is here with me in spirit.
Neither time nor place
could tear us apart completely.

CLAIRE

I will draw the world we once spoke of,
as we hid amongst the shadows of this beach,
when the dark crept its way in.

I must head home now
and draw ...

Act 1, Scene 6

DORIS
Now you are all treated.
All that is needed is rest.

CITIZENS
Bless you, Madam Hospitaller.

DORIS
Tell me, how close is our enemy?

CITIZENS
Close. Their breath is on our necks.

DORIS
Last night I heard the bombs in the distance.
Luckily we weren't hit.

CITIZENS
Not yet.

DORIS
You are saying we do not have much time?

CITIZENS
No, we do not.

You say your daughter has not seen the
devastation outside that front door?

DORIS
No. Nor will she.

All that she suffers inside these walls is enough.

CITIZENS
You wish to protect her?

DORIS
Yes. No matter how much this house crumbles,
she will not leave it.

Her childhood dreams will keep her entertained.

CITIZENS

Is it not better to make her aware of the truth?
It might prepare her for the worst.

DORIS

The worst has already happened.
My son ...

CITIZENS

What happened Madam?

DORIS

One evening he was in the living room,
the next minute he was gone.

There's a hole in the wall.

He must have slipped through.

I searched for so long, up and down the streets,
through this house.

I could not find him.

Every day I pray, many times.

I fear for his life.

CITIZENS

How does your daughter cope?

DORIS

She does not sleep much.
She finds it difficult to understand
that her brother has gone.
She speaks about him as though he is still here.

I will let you sleep.
Rest well.

CITIZENS

It is a strange event to occur
for a boy to suddenly disappear.
No trace in the streets or house itself.

Where he is now remains a mystery.

CITIZENS

How to find the missing boy?
The war-torn streets have shed many a life.
Each broken body nameless until claimed.
All victims of another being's strife.

Alas, this woman cannot shelter her child
forever from the angry fire.
The enemy's breath is on our necks.
Devastation will strike the innocent.

Act 1, Scene 7

SAMUEL

The breath of this world is bountiful,
exhaling its life in abundance across the plain.
I see the first shoots of new grass,
beginning to unfurl themselves into large stalks,
that shift and bend in the slightly elevated breeze.

It is odd that they grow here
as there is no clear light shining.
Day and night seem to have morphed into one,
leaving a stark stillness of anticipation.

What will happen next?

Staring up now, I absorb the dim light,
letting it saturate my wide, wakeful eyes.

I my mind's eye, I can see my sister, Claire.
She is staring at me, with her intense, green eyes.

Now I remember ...

CLAIRE

Can you see it, Samuel?
The rainbow, outside?

SAMUEL

Yes. Shining so brightly,
in defiance of the battle
that has consumed this world.

Impermanent yet here, it shines,
reflecting the most beautiful shades.

CLAIRE

A colour is missing.
It has gone away for now.

SAMUEL

What do you mean?
I see red, yellow, pink, green, orange, violet ...

CLAIRE

Hiding away it is,
so tired of not being seen.

One day, it will come back,
shining brightly.
You will see.

SAMUEL

I'm sorry, Claire, that we have to live
through such dangerous moments.
Deep in my heart, I hope with all my might
that things will become better again.

CLAIRE

It's good to hope, Samuel.
It carries light.

Hold your hands together, like this.

SAMUEL

Alright.
What am I doing?

CLAIRE

Close your eyes, tightly.

Whisper what you hope for
and wave your hands in the air, like this.

SAMUEL

My mind is drifting, considering
my body, my presence, in this moment.

Just a small speck, I am,
amongst all the fiery rage.
I am not sure that my wishes would even
make the smallest impact on anything.

CLAIRE

We must fight for our hopes, Samuel,
they are too precious to lose.
If we carry enough hope, we can heal the world.

So, let this light carry our hopes
and dress the world in bright colours,
just like this alluring rainbow.

SAMUEL

What a touching thought, Claire.
It can't hurt to hope,
yet fill our souls with light.

Let's do that.

Maybe somewhere, in the aether, our hopes may be heard.

Dissipating, are your eyes, Claire,
as though I am awakening from a dream.

I know that it wasn't.

I know that you are here with me.

In my mind, you are still smiling, like you always have.

Your gentle, reassuring smile of knowing
that everything will be okay.

I believe in you.

Staring up at the light, still,
I begin to understand what you mean, Claire.
It is so dull, this light.

A colour is clearly missing.
Possibly one that is not visible
to the naked, human eye.

Maybe it will make its way
here in this new world.

Maybe it may even bring
you and Mother back to me.

Act 1, Scene 8

CLAIRE
It is dark.
I exhale fog.
The window is steamy.

Wipe it away.

Let's see outside.

People are running, very fast.
They are very scared.
Where are they going?

Hello?
Can I help you?

Block your ears!
The air raid calls!

A haunting sound
that I want to disappear.

No more darkness Mother.
We must keep our eyes open.

DORIS
It's an air raid!

Claire, turn out that light!

CLAIRE
Why Mother?
It's too dark.

DORIS
Claire, the lamp!

CLAIRE
The light is snuffed out.

Mother?
The people outside are running very fast.
They are scared.
Can I help?

DORIS
No!
Stay still.

CLAIRE
It's too dark!

DORIS
Hit the ground, Claire!
We're under attack!

CLAIRE
No more fire!

DORIS
Claire! Are you alright?

Is everyone alright?

CLAIRE
No more fire, Mother!

DORIS
It's okay.
It's over now.
Help me check on our visitors, Claire.

CLAIRE
Fire hurts.
Fire takes people away!

We must hide.

Where is the paper?
I must draw ...

CITIZENS
– Bless you Madam.
– Just a small leg wound to heal.
– Are you injured, Madam?

DORIS
I am fine.
There are some repairs needed before we can sleep.
The furniture is destroyed.
The wall is beginning to cave in.

CITIZENS
Let us help you, Madam.

CLAIRE
We must hide.
No more fire.

Time to draw now.

Grass must bring life.

Act 1, Scene 9

SAMUEL
I am walking across the paper grassland,
admiring remnant sparks of fire
still aglow on the tips of grass blades.

Protectors, they are, of this land,
like eyes, seeing through the darkness.

The red and orange hues of dawn
are slowly revealing the new day.
Up high, just for a moment,
I watch as a cloud transforms into a heart shape.
Within it, are two, bright green eyes
and a warm, toothy grin.

Claire is here with me in spirit.

The light rays are not very strong,
yet they warm my body a little.
Reaching toward the rays,
I silently connect with my sister.
Tears of gratitude roll down my cheeks.

Staring down, I gaze once more at the grassland.
Inhaling a breath of surprise,
I watch as the sparks of fire
begin to transform into new growth.

Parsley, chives and basil are sprouting
between the grass blades, alive and fragrant.

I can hear a rustling sound through the grass
and bob down, hiding away.

From this distance, I see a cat like creature,
with long, shiny gold fur,
large whiskers and pointed ears,
walking across the grass.

YARROW
I muzt be quick.
Light iz fadin'
2 sprigz of parzley,
4 pine needlez.
1 orange.

YARROW

Yez, 1 violet petal.
Clawz are full.

Enuff 'erbz and flowerz.
Time to make a zleepin' draught.
2 'ealth tonicz and
1 remedy for a leg wound.
Yarrow helpz people feel bedda.

Zometink'z not right.
Woz dat noize?

Dere feet prez inta bark.
Clozer now.

Dey iz comin'!
Quick! Zhake da pine tree!

Got ya pine cone!

Ya zhine bright light.
It 'elpz Yarrow zee bedda.

Dey is arfta zometink.
Zometink new.
It 'az brung da fire wit it.

Iz Zamuel.

I zee ya.

Ya've arrived.

Act 1, Scene 10

CLAIRE
No more food, Mother?
I'm hungry.

DORIS
Just some lettuce leaves
and one tomato.

I'm hungry too.

CLAIRE
Have mine, Mother.

DORIS
I've already eaten. It's for you.

Eat slowly Claire.
It's to last you all day.

There must be a way to get some
more food.

CITIZENS
There is a way, Madam.

DORIS
There is?

CITIZENS
Yes, at the new food distribution office,
there is a ration service.

DORIS
Are you able to help us?

Can you get us some food?

CITIZENS
No Madam.
Only the head of the family can sign up for the service.

DORIS
I have to go outside?

CITIZENS

You can't avoid the reality forever.
Seeing will keep you informed.

DORIS

I must go or my daughter will starve.

Please look after Claire while I am gone.

Under no circumstances should you let her outside.

CITIZENS

Of course Madam.

CLAIRE

Where are you going, Mother?
Can I come?

DORIS

No. Finish your food.
You must stay inside.
It's not safe.

I am going now.

Take care, Claire.

CLAIRE

Mother!
Let me come with you!
I will take care of you!

Act 1, Scene 11

DORIS

A thick, grey haze filters through the air,
remnants of the fire of wrath
that blasted its way through the night.

Morning it is, yet is not,
the sun hiding its cautious rays
behind the strong smoke of anger.

CLAIRE

I want to go outside!

CITIZENS

It breaks one's heart to see the girl
imprisoned in the confines of these walls.
How she must wish to stretch her legs
and play in the world outside.

CLAIRE

I will save Mother from the dark!
She must hide.

CITIZENS

Hide? Where should she hide?

CLAIRE

In the grass.
Tall grass under a shining sun.

I will hide there too.

CITIZENS

Will she be safe there?

CLAIRE

Yes, fire won't find her.

DORIS

Rage on, anger will,
be it day or night,
an existence that has emptied me
of light's vibrancy.

DORIS

A walking shadow I have become.
My soul's pockets empty of life.

I see my shadow now,
flittering closely behind me,
determined to follow my trails
into the encroaching darkness.

My feet, when lifted, leave patterns
of life once walked upon Maren's grounds.
Patterns I long to retrace and rediscover,
in the beauty of Lady Solary's light.

I once thrived in her light,
my body taller and carrying me confidently.
A wife, I was, to my loving husband, Ray.
A home we made with our beautiful children.

Honest lives we lived,
in the security of Maren's embrace.

Yet now, Maren has changed.

Foreign are my footprints now,
striking so cautiously across the ground.

I am without husband,
my soul yearning to save my daughter from the war.

Be the hope you wish to see.

I remember those words,
once shared with me by Ray,
as the darkness of the war crept in on us.

Watch my shadow, I can now,
as it twirls independently,
away from my body.

Dancing, my shadow is now,
along with yours, Ray.
Embracing and twirling they are,
like we used to at dusk.

My shadow still follows me.
It has seen all there is,
a reliable companion,
through the light and the dark.

DORIS

My shadow carries me now, pushing my
exhausted frame along,
through smoke's chalky haze.

I see ...

foreign, dark shadows moving swiftly,
in and out of the rays of light.
Hiding they are, waiting for their chance
to catch our world by surprise.

Eyes, I see,
two eyes, unblinking
and tormented,
appearing from a shadow.

Eyes that belong to the *other*.

Approaching me are those eyes,
along with short, black hair
and a twisted, scary smile.

Running I am now, quickly,
dragging my own shadow of hope
directly behind my fatigued frame.

Bobbing behind a market stall,
I inhale short, sharp breaths,
waiting for the inevitable sound ...

Fire strikes the air now,
the wrath of single gun shots,
aiming for what enemy lies in its reach.

Huddling I am now,
burying my head in my arms,
trying to wipe the sound away.

I cannot afford to die here.

My children need their mother.

The gunfire has ceased for now.
The tension has lifted.

My body is shaking
and my tears are falling.

Peering behind the market stall,
I check for *them*.
All clear.

DORIS

I am alone.

My shadow is reaching
across the darkness for you, Ray.

Can you feel its energy?

SAMUEL

There you are!

DORIS

Who is that?
Oh, it's another shadow.
It's dark, I can't make out its shape.

SAMUEL

You can't find me, Mother!

DORIS

Your voice is so real, so alive.
Don't look around you, son.
This world is not one you should face.

Just look into my eyes,
I will keep you safe.

CITIZENS

The Mist will watch over your mother.

CLAIRE

Mist!

CITIZENS

Mist unbound,
spanning towards the horizon.

Lady Solary will bless our saviours
who protect us from danger.

OFFICIAL VOICE

Move along, please Madam.
It's not safe to loiter in the streets.
Curfew is not too far away.

DORIS

Have you seen my son, Officer?
He is this high,
with dark hair and a lovely smile.

Last time I saw him,
we were playing hide and seek.
You know, he can play that game forever!

OFFICIAL VOICE

No Madam,
I have not seen a child of that description.

What's his name?

DORIS

Samuel.

OFFICIAL VOICE

You're from Gibrati Street, aren't you?

DORIS

How do you – ?

OFFICIAL VOICE

It's our job to know where everyone is, Madam.

DORIS

Why are you standing in your shadow?
I can't see your face!

OFFICIAL VOICE

I am very busy, Mrs Attard.

DORIS

Mrs Attard!

OFFICIAL VOICE

If you just give me a moment,
I will accompany you to the ...
food distribution office?

DORIS

No need! Thank you!

You just keep tending to your business!
I will get there myself!

SAMUEL

Mother, come find me!

DORIS

10, 9, 8, 7... Where are you Samuel?
You were always so good at hiding.
I know you're out here somewhere.

Arriving at the food distribution office.

Signing up for the service, distracted.

Watching Samuel disappear around a corner.
His face is bright and smiling.

I'm counting now, Samuel!

6. Soap.
5. Sugar.
4. Bread.
3. Pasta.
2. Matches.
1. Kerosene.

Ready or not!
Here I come to find you!

SAMUEL

Ssh Mother!
It's a secret!

DORIS

Watch that hole, Samuel!
Don't disappear through there!
It's dangerous!

SAMUEL

I'm not scared Mother!
I'll protect you!
Come find me!

DORIS

Samuel! I'm here son!
Samuel?

He's gone.

SUSAN MARSHALL

CITIZENS
The mist smothers fire.
It hovers in the sky,
keeping watch over us
and drives away our enemy.

CLAIRE
Healing mist.

I must draw now.

The mist floats in the sky
and the world shines once more.

See my picture?
We are all smiling.
There is no more darkness.

CITIZENS
For this precious moment in time
our pain is trivial and forgotten.
As we allow the innocent voice of a girl
bless us with hope and vision.

Lady Solary, we see your light
at presence within this steadfast girl.
Let it subdue the most ready weapon
and awaken the conscience within.

Act 1, Scene 12

CLAIRE
Mother, you're home!

DORIS
Let me sit for a moment.
Go play, Claire.

CITIZENS
Are you alright Madam?

DORIS
I fear that Lady Solary has abandoned us forever.

CITIZENS
That is not possible, Madam.

DORIS
Then why doesn't she strike *them*?

CITIZENS
The streets are cluttered, aren't they?

It is nearly on your doorstep, Madam.
You can't escape it forever.

DORIS
Don't you think I know that?
Our peoples' bodies continue to fall.
Are we next?

Lady Solary, where do you hide?
Why do you leave us to suffer?

CITIZENS
Perhaps it is you that has changed, Madam.
A hardened heart will not allow
the light of Lady Solary to prosper.

You can learn a lot from your daughter.

DORIS
My daughter?
What could she possibly teach me
about surviving the war?

Or about how to escape this constant nightmare?

The images I see ...

CITIZENS
What images are they, Madam?

DORIS

My son, all alone out there, needing his mother.

I can never seem to reach him.

It would be a miracle if he was still alive.

What must we do to be blessed
with your guidance, Lady Solary?

CITIZENS
Lady Solary is guiding you, Madam.

DORIS
Guiding me? How?
Is she choosing to make me suffer?

CIVILIANS
Not at all.

DORIS.
Time to unpack.

Kerosene.
Where's that lamp?

CITIZENS
A change of mindset is what you need
to reconnect once more with Lady Solary.

The answer lies right in front of your eyes
yet you do not see it.

DORIS
Sugar, bread ... matches ...
Where's those matches?

CITIZENS

It would not harm you to pause, Madam.
Watch what is happening before your eyes
and discover the choices that you have.

DORIS

Choices? During a war?
We are surrounded by brutality.

Our choices are to live or to die.

CITIZENS

Ask yourself this question, Madam:
how do you wish to live?

DORIS

What is your answer to that question?

CIVILIANS

We have made our choice Madam.

We thank you for your hospitality,
however soon we will leave and
face the fortune that life provides us with.

DORIS

A very brave choice.
Best of luck to you.

Matches ... I need to find those matches.

Act 1, Scene 13

CLAIRE
Matchsticks!

This matchstick is Dahren.
This one is Trisha,
Anthony and
Ayarna.

DORIS
I thought I put the box of matchsticks on the table ...

Claire, what are you doing with my matches?

CLAIRE
Fire is bad.

DORIS
Is that so?

CLAIRE
Yes.
Fire takes people away.

Mother, these matchsticks are:
Dahren, Trisha, Anthony and Ayarna.

DORIS
Our dear visitors.
You've learnt their names.

Bless your loving heart, Claire.

CLAIRE
These people need new clothes.

DORIS
Clothes, eh?
I have just the thing for you.
The latest Sewer's Dream catalogue.

See? Clothes you can cut out yourself.
You can wrap them around these small matchsticks.

CLAIRE

Lots of clothes.

DORIS

Here are the scissors.

I will have to find some more matches, Claire.
You seem to have used quite a few of them.

CLAIRE

It's fun to dress people in new clothes.

Dahren, Trisha, Anthony and Ayarna,
you are beautiful people in this world.
A warmth exudes from you, even in this state,
unlit yet ready to set alight in a new world.

I place you all on this picture now …

Act 2, Scene 1

MIST

Past citizens we are of Amarinda,
healed by the hospitaller woman.
Wise from the consequences of rage,
our voices have promised to keep silent.

A young girl's stroke has breathed us life
upon this luscious, grassy meadow.
Unbound we float in the aether,
protecting the sanctuary of life below.

To grow, this world needs nurturing
only Lady Solary's warmth can provide.
Yet light flickers briefly then fades,
like a struck match failing to ignite.

Buried deep within a pure soul,
Lady Solary plans a new world of life.
Her future power entirely depends
on a mother's belief in her child.

YARROW

Lookz like cloud down low.

SAMUEL

It's a mist.
So beautiful.
The pine trees look silver.
I cannot see too far beyond them.

Put your paw out Yarrow.
That's it.
Feel the water droplets against your fur.
It's safe, I promise.

YARROW

Iz woter?

SAMUEL

Yes. For it to have developed,
there has to be a water source nearby.

YARROW

Iz gettin' dark.

Me grab a pine cone.

Zee? Cone lightz up!
Iz bedda.

SAMUEL

Why is this world so dark?
Daylight comes and goes so quickly.

YARROW

Yez. Da way it 'az alwayz been.

SAMUEL

Always? How do you grow things?

YARROW

Iz 'ard. Wen zky zhinez, 'erbz grow.
Den dey wilt up and die wen dark.
Yarrow muz be quick ta gader de 'erbz
before dey're gone.

Wotz dat zound?

SAMUEL

Don't be afraid, Yarrow.
Nothing is going to hurt you, I promise.
Hold my hand and follow me down this track.

YARROW

I don' won'ta zee.

SAMUEL

Wow!

It's so majestic.

Look at the power of the water,
plummeting to the floor below.
It can course its way through anything.

Yarrow?
You can open your eyes now.

Have you seen a waterfall before, Yarrow?

YARROW
Nah.

SAMUEL
Enchanting, isn't it?

YARROW
'nchant?

SAMUEL
Like magic.
This is where the mist has come from.
See?

YARROW
It woz not 'ere before.
Y'ave brung't 'ere.

SAMUEL
You think I've brought it here?

YARROW
Zamuel iz da one we've been told'll come.
Ya'll 'elp uz.

SAMUEL
Help you? How?

YARROW
Ta live in dis world dat iz new.
Ta know how ta uze it.
We do not know wot we need to grow and zurvive.

Will ya 'elp uz?

SAMUEL
Of course. It would be an honour to help.
I'm afraid I'm not much of a fighter though.

YARROW
Datz fine, Zamuel.
Neither iz our people, dey're 'urt.

SAMUEL
Hurt?
Yarrow, what's going on?

YARROW

Evry day more 'nd more people come 'ere 'urt.
Zome of dem we do not know.

Dere iz a dark forze amung uz we call *dem*.
We do not dare go too far outzide da pine treez.

SAMUEL

That's why you gather herbs?
To heal your people?

YARROW

Yez. Now Yarrow can 'elp da people.
But zoon dere'll be too many.
Yarrow be zent to find a medizine person.

SAMUEL

You mean a person to help fix injuries and heal the sick?
Like a doctor?

YARROW

Yez. Yarrow only crush and mix 'erbz
to make remediez for da people.

SAMUEL

I see.

YARROW

're ya medizine person, Samuel?

SAMUEL

Me? No, not at all.
I know someone who is though.

YARROW

Ya do?

SAMUEL

Yes.

YARROW

Zamuel 'elp Yarrow?

SAMUEL
Yes. But first of all, we must eat.

See the still water at the bottom of the waterfall?

YARROW
Yez.

SAMUEL
We can swim in that, hunt for fish.
What do you say?

YARROW
Fiz'?

SAMUEL
I will show you.

You just need to step into the water,
that's right.

YARROW
Iz cool,
wavez up to hipz.

Iz deep.

SAMUEL
Step carefully now.
Great work, Yarrow!

Are you hungry?

YARROW
Yarrow iz very 'ungry.

SAMUEL
Time to catch some fish!

Act 2, Scene 2

CLAIRE
Mother!
Look at my picture!

DORIS
Wow! Grass?

CLAIRE
Yes.

DORIS
Is that fog?

CLAIRE
Mist.

DORIS
It's hard to see through.

CLAIRE
Mother, see the surprise!
Look! Behind the mist!

DORIS
Why, it's a waterfall.
What a beautiful feature, Claire.

CLAIRE
Pretty waterfall.
See the cave?

DORIS
Oh, yes.
Who lives in the cave?

CLAIRE
The people of the land.
First they hid in the grass
and now many hide in the cave,
away from the bad fire.

Do you want to hide in the cave, too, Mother?

DORIS

I wish it was that easy, Claire
and the world was that beautiful.

You stuck matchsticks on there too.
What are they for, Claire?

CLAIRE

They are Dahren, Trisha, Anthony and Ayarna.

DORIS

Our old guests.

CLAIRE

There's Samuel.

DORIS

Your dear brother, bless his heart.
I miss him too, Claire.

I wish we could find him.

CLAIRE

Hide in the grass, Samuel.
Dark won't find you.

DORIS

So, that's where all my matches have gone ...

For now, I must repaint the
black on the windows to protect us, Claire.

CLAIRE

The mist must protect the world
from danger, too.

I must draw ...

Act 2, Scene 3

MIST

Oh what heart the young girl has
to provide the people with a waterfall.
The sound of cascading water roars
as it descends from a magnificent height.

Deep within the shallow streams,
lies much to be hunted and devoured.
The people will learn new ways of life
along the banks and harbour of the river.

Across the mountains and planes
we float and build a protective haze.
The sounds of distant, enemy gunfire
growing stronger as each day passes.

The young girl's pencil stroke stops us
outside the entry to a deep, dark cave.
Peering down upon the world, we see
a land undefined and yet to be claimed.

Below the grassland blooms once more
with violet, hyssop and lavender.
Limestone gleams along the cave walls,
an essential treasure yet to be discovered.

In a circle we hover, creating a barrier,
limiting *their* visibility of the land below.

SAMUEL

The exotic, green sand draws my attention,
its trail luring me closer towards the
open mouth of a magnificent cave.

I am pressing my palm gently against the coraline limestone.
It feels warm against my skin, alerting me to
my own physical presence in this moment.
My body exists right here, right now.

I feel the rare, radiant rays of the sun,
warming my neck and back.
Steady the light is, not fading away this time.

SAMUEL
I am reaching towards the sun.
A source of comfort and reassurance.
I swear I can see Claire's face in its luminescence.
She is smiling at me.

YARROW
Ya ready, Zamuel?

SAMUEL
We are lucky to be alive, you and I.

We can walk and talk,
roam this land.

YARROW
Yez.

Zome not zo lucky, Zamuel.

SAMUEL
A strong shadow has cast itself,
like a dark veil of sadness,
blocking the soothing rays of the sun.

Surrounded by the shadow's thick cloak,
my view of the world is tinier,
zoning in on the darkness I inhabit.

I am being sucked into the dark,
unable to release its strong grasp of me.
My heart pounds like a storm
as I try to wrestle against the blackness.

Narrower, the world becomes still,
like a twisting, dark tunnel of silence.

A powerful silence, that lures me
to take one step, then another,
through the mouth of the big cave.

Hanging from a limestone wall,
is a single, burning torch light,
enabling me to see before me.

Many, many bones are strewn
across the sandy, cave floor.
Historical remnants of creatures
who once trekked and resided here.

SAMUEL

It is sad to consider life's impermanency.
To touch the world with one's
special grace and to then leave it ...
behind.

I miss my father all the time,
his dark absence smothers my heart
and leaves me breathless.

Where are you Father?
I hope you are safe.
Mother is doing all she
can to look after us both.

Other mothers and their children
hide here in this very darkness.

Some children are being comforted
and fed the tiniest amount of food.

One woman rocks her body in the corner,
her lips pressed tightly together in pain
as she clutches at her injured arm.

A tight, small space of refuge
houses these brave women and children.

They share the same latrine,
a small hole dug into the sand.

Silent, they all are, so solemn,
trying to live out their days.
They sit within the dark shadows,
waiting, just like I am now.

Bodies are marked with stains
of their ventures across the terrain.

Some bodies are barely clothed
and huddle together for warmth.

A child's gaze meets mine.

Wide eyed, she is, her eyes full of hope.

Biting my lip, I search for the right words.

I am here for you.

I will do my best to help you all get better.

SAMUEL

The darkness is lifting away,
pulling me backwards out of the cave.

It is light again and the sun's rays are welcome.

YARROW

Ready ta 'elp, Zamuel?

SAMUEL

Yes.

I am going to use some of this limestone
from this magnificent cave
to build a clinic.

Would you like to help, Yarrow?

YARROW

Yez!

SAMUEL

We should build the foundations first.
I will need a hammer, shovel and chisel.

YARROW

Dey is ova dere.

SAMUEL

Wow! A pile of limestone at my feet, too?
This land is full of surprises!

Now, how big is this space?

1 step, 2 steps, 3 steps...

Yarrow? Where are you?

YARROW

Zzh! Can you 'ear dat?

SAMUEL

Yes.

MIST

The enemy's breath is on our necks,
approaching rapidly in the night ether.
A dangerous shape from back home,
interfering with this beautiful place.

SAMUEL

I know this sound. I've heard it before.
It's an air raid.

YARROW

Zcary zound!
Mizt, 'elp uz!

MIST

The dark shadow looms behind us,
approaching in its horrendous form.
Large wings and body, a fighter jet,
scouting for the enemy to burn.

SAMUEL

Get into the cave, Yarrow, quickly!
There's not much time!

YARROW

Iz diz de end Zamuel?

SAMUEL

The ground's shaking!
Yarrow, hold onto something solid!

YARROW

Wot iz dat?
Iz a very dark zhadow.

SAMUEL

An enemy from another world.
It's shaped like a fighter plane.
Strange it's here though.
What does it want?

YARROW

Dey wont evry ting dey can get.
Dey don't underztand peace.
Our home'll be deztroy'd.

SAMUEL

Time to focus now, Yarrow.
Hold on tight!

MIST

The tremoring ground alerts the conscience
to the safety of the world it inhabits.
Grouping together and forming a haze
We Mist rise, obstructing the enemy's vision.

The shaking subsides,
the pressure is released.
We hold still, not trusting the silence.

SAMUEL

It's alright Yarrow,
the shaking has stopped.
You can let go now.

YARROW

Dey iz ztill 'ere Zamuel.
I can feel dere prezence.

SAMUEL

You can?

MIST

The enemy has landed.
5 seconds ...
15 seconds ...
40 seconds ...

Feet snap against bark.

Shapes approach our haze,
desperate to break through the barrier.

YARROW

Dere iz not much time now Zamuel.
Dey're comin'!

'Tiz up to Our Lady now.

Act 2, Scene 4

DORIS
Samuel?

CLAIRE
Mother!
The door bell is ringing!

OFFICIAL VOICE
Anyone in there?
Mrs Attard?

DORIS
Ssh!

Stay away from the windows, Claire.
It's not safe.

Come and sit with me.

OFFICIAL VOICE
Mrs Attard?
Please answer the door.

If you can hear me Mrs Attard,
I am from the army services.
We are asking, no requesting,
everyone to evacuate.

CLAIRE
We must leave, Mother.

OFFICIAL VOICE
Mrs Attard?
This area is in grave danger of -

DORIS
That's enough! I heard you!

Go away!
We're not going anywhere!

OFFICIAL VOICE

It's no time to be a hero, Mrs Attard.
You have a young daughter in there, yes?

The people are gathering underground at the city train station.
We suggest you make the right decision.

We'll return in the morning to check that you have left.

CLAIRE

Did the dark find us, Mother?

Are there more broken bodies?

I can help you, Mother.

We must leave now!

DORIS

We're not leaving until your brother returns, Claire.

CLAIRE

Samuel returns?
Samuel is hiding.
I told you where he is.

DORIS

There's no time for fantasies, Claire!
Do you have any idea what it's like outside?

CLAIRE

Yes, I knows it is very dark,
like a nightmare.

I will show you a brighter world.
I must find my picture ...

DORIS

All is safe for now.

Samuel, why won't you return to us?

Act 2, Scene 5

MIST

The noise of the enemy is deafening
as it beats against our guarded veil.
Attempting to push through our barrier,
they wish to attack and claim the land as theirs.

There is no longer any time to wait.
Lady Solary's light will only shine with belief.
There is one last step that does remain
before this new world will be free from harm.

CLAIRE

I need one more matchstick.

Where are you, matchstick?

MIST

Gunshots blast, piercing our veil.

We hold each other with all our might.

CLAIRE

I crave the light.
The windows are so black.
It's so dark!

Who is outside Mother?

Angry fire!

DORIS

The air raid!
Claire!

Where are you?
Claire?

MIST

Swaying in the aether, we fight for life.
For the future, for the –

CLAIRE
Block your ears!
Another haunting air raid calls!

Grown ups should not play with fire.
Fire takes people away.

We must hide.

Matchstick!

DORIS
Claire, leave the matchstick!
It's not time for games.

Into the centre of the room, quick!

CLAIRE
Time to roll out the picture.
It is ready now.

This matchstick is you, Mother!

Mother, you light this match!

DORIS
Claire, don't be silly!

Please, just come to the centre of the room!

Come to your mother, please!

CLAIRE
If you do not light this match,
I will not come.

Please Mother, do it for all of us?

MIST
We draw in sharp, painful breaths,
bracing ourselves against the onslaught.
Protecting the world with all our might.
Hoping for the right answer ...

DORIS
You children and your games!

CLAIRE
Mother!
I promise this is not a game.

DORIS

Alright.
I'll light the match.

CLAIRE

Now say your name.

DORIS

Oh Claire, please!

Alright.
Doris.

CLAIRE

Now hold my hand.

DORIS

I've got you now, come on.
Game's over.

CLAIRE

Step on the picture!

Mother!
Let me save you!

MIST

Time slows in this terrifying moment.
We can no longer hold up against the blasts.
Our veil begins to crumble and we fall.
Please, let the right decision be made...

CLAIRE

You stepped on the picture, Mother!
I am standing with you, see?

Now hold my hand, tightly!

Act 2, Scene 6

SAMUEL

I wake to silence.
It's so unusual.

No need to move yet.
I am safe.

The air is thick with mist.
It conceals me from *them*.
Faint pencil lines of pine trees
are visible in the distance.

YARROW

Ya in da plaze ya mean'ta be, Zamuel.

SAMUEL

Yes I am.
There is no more angry fire.

YARROW

Nah, iz peazeful.

SAMUEL

Do you see the bright, white light,
shining across the mist?

It's getting stronger by the second!

YARROW

I zee it.
It iz time.

MIST

Claire's bright, indigo light reflects
through our water droplets.

SAMUEL

A light of hope!
It shines so beautifully,
reaching out towards us.

We might just be saved, Yarrow.

MIST

Lingering in the air, we disperse,
allowing a gap for a mother to pass.
She is bruised, battered, yet a fighter,
still searching for her long lost son.

DORIS

My boy, where are you?

SAMUEL

There's a figure, walking through the mist.
In this light, so far is very close.

Time to move... away from *them!*

I am running,
my feet dragging through the grass.

YARROW

Ztop Zamuel!
No need ta hide now!

Dey iz gone.

Look cloza.

SAMUEL

Really? I'm so tired of hiding.

That figure, it looks very familiar,
from another time and place.

Is it who I think it is?

MIST

The light shines even brighter,
allowing us to float higher,
dispersing in the aether,
keeping watch over the world.

YARROW

Da grazz is pickin' itzelf up.
Da 'erbz are unfurlin'.
Da zhape is pickin' da 'erbz.

SAMUEL

And so she is,
with her gentle, healing hands …

Mother!

YARROW

Don't dizturb her, Zamuel.
Zhe haz jus' arrived.

DORIS

Claire? Come down from the trees.
I have found the herbs and flowers.
We can heal ourselves now.

CLAIRE

Yes Mother.
See my light shining?

DORIS

Yes. How beautiful!

Oh Claire!
Lady Solary's spirit shines within you.

CLAIRE

No more darkness, Mother!
The world shines with so much hope.

Some people are hurt.
Will you help them?

DORIS

Of course!
I just need to pick some more of this parsley and aloe vera.

Is there any dandelion?

CLAIRE

Here Mother.

DORIS

I didn't see that!
Where was that hiding?

CLAIRE

In the grass, Mother.

Anything else?

DORIS

This will do for now.
I will need to crush these to make medicine.

Act 2, Scene 7

CLAIRE
Yarrow?

YARROW
Our Lady of Light!
Yarrow bowz for ya.

CLAIRE
Oh Yarrow!

The grass, herbs and trees.
The waterfall and caves ...

The picture is alive!

YARROW
Yez, my Lady, it iz.
Just az you dezigned it.

CLAIRE
You have taken great care of this world, both of you.
Thank you.

SAMUEL
Claire, you told me the truth.
I was right to believe you.

You carry Lady Solary within you.

You shine a light that is so hard to see
by the human eye, yet here it is.
Bright, indigo light.
The missing colour of the rainbow.

I remember ...

Running around the corner,
away from Mother,
playing hide and seek.

Seeing you Claire,
in our dark, confined living room.

Wanting to show me the picture.
Making me a promise ...

CLAIRE

Hide in the grass!
Dark won't find you!

I will meet you in the light.

SAMUEL

Here we are, under rays of indigo,
both alive and breathing.

Mother is safe too.

You helped us to escape the war?

CLAIRE

Yes. No more darkness.

SAMUEL

You saved our lives.

CLAIRE

You are safe now, in the light.
So is Mother.

We now live in the world that Father and I
planned for our healing and refuge.

We are safe and free from danger.

SAMUEL

Dear Father, I miss him so much.

May he find peace in knowing that we are safe now.

For the first time in a long time,
I feel at peace.

No more running away from *them*.

This is quite the haven, Claire.

CLAIRE

Haven?

SAMUEL

It is our new home, we are safe here.
You have created a masterpiece.

CLAIRE

Haven.

SAMUEL

We have a lot of people to care for.

I am building a clinic.

CLAIRE

The people will love it Samuel.

You are a boy with a big heart.

Act 2, Scene 8

DORIS

10, 9, 8, 7... Where are you Samuel?
You were always so good at hiding.
I know you're out here somewhere.

SAMUEL

Hiding behind a solitary, clinic wall.

Can you find me, Mother?
I'm not too far away now!

DORIS

6, 5, 4, 3, 2, 1...

A building under construction.

Are you here, Samuel?

SAMUEL

You've nearly found me, Mother!

DORIS

Hello young boy.

Are you unwell?

I see you are holding yourself up, there.

SAMUEL

Hello Mother.

DORIS

Samuel!

My dear son!
I knew you were alive!

Let me hold you.

You've grown, son.

SAMUEL

Yes I have.
So has Claire.

DORIS

Are you building this, Samuel?
It's beautiful.

SAMUEL

Yes, it's a clinic.

You can see that we have a lot of work to do.

The people will need your medical expertise.

DORIS

I am always happy to help those who need it, Samuel.

SAMUEL

Let me introduce you to Yarrow.

YARROW

Very pleaze ta meet ya, Madam.

DORIS

Lovely to meet you, too, Yarrow.

YARROW

Da people'll be very 'appy Madam.
Dey been prayin' for ya t'arrive.

DORIS

I'd better prepare some medicine.

Is there a mortar and pestle here?
I need to crush these herbs.

YARROW

Yarrow'll do dat, Madam.

DORIS

Why, thank you Yarrow.

SAMUEL

Do you remember how you got here, Mother?

DORIS

No. Strange as it is, the last thing I remember
is waiting for Claire to return with a picture.

SAMUEL

The picture? What did it look like?

DORIS

I vaguely remember mist and grass.
I can't remember all the details.
She is quite the talented artist.

SAMUEL

Yes, she always has been.

You are standing in the picture right now, Mother.

DORIS

I am? That is not possible!

SAMUEL

Come outside.
Let me show you.

Act 2, Scene 9

CLAIRE
Tall pine tree, Samuel!
We must balance.

SAMUEL
Hold my hand,
let me help you up.

CLAIRE
You are a fast climber.

SAMUEL
I've been wanting to hug a tree trunk for so long.

It is great to climb again!

What did you want me to see, Claire?

CLAIRE
Look, over here!

SAMUEL
At the mist?
I could see that from the ground.

CLAIRE
Hello Mist!

MIST
You are glowing, Claire.

We see Lady Solary's spirit shining through you.

It is an honour to be in your presence, Our Lady.

CLAIRE
Are you hurt, Mist?

MIST
A little hurt.
Yet we will slowly heal on our own.

CLAIRE

You saved Samuel from *them*.
Thank you Mist.

SAMUEL

I owe you my life, Mist.
Thank you.

MIST

To see you safe and free is all that matters.

CLAIRE

I am outside, Mist!

MIST

Yes, you finally are, with such a radiant smile.

What more will you provide?

CLAIRE

Freedom for Mist.

You helped us.
Now you are free to go.

MIST

We thank you for the offer, Claire.
However, long ago we made our choice.
We remain in this ethereal form,
willing to protect the life forms around us.

We Mist are now unbound,
spanning outwards towards the horizon.

CLAIRE

What an honour to have you stay with us, Mist!

Thank you Mist.

MIST

From this very moment in time,
past pain is trivial and forgotten.
We allow the wise voice of a girl
to bless us with hope and vision.

SAMUEL

Race your light to the bottom of the tree, Claire!

CLAIRE

Mist floats in the sky.
The world shines.

See? We are free.
No more fire.
No more darkness.

MIST

We will always be with you,
protecting you in this haven.

Lady Solary we see your beaming light,
present within this steadfast girl.
May this light subdue the most ready weapon
by enlightening good conscience within.

The End.

Other books in the groundbreaking, *Theatre Playscapes* series:

*"The carnation flower's scent is fragrant in the breeze.
It wakes me so I escape the dark world of dreams."*

Awakening on the golden flower bridge of Bry, Fleur cannot remember how she came to be there. There are lingering fumes of smoke in the air and within her reach, lies her romantic partner, Sherwin's jacket. Wrapped around Fleur's wrist is a living, wild Carnation flower.

Determined to find answers, Fleur travels back in time with the wild Carnation flower. As she revisits moments of yesterday, she engages with the living energies of her lifeworld. Slowly, Fleur unravels the lingering, dark mystery behind Sherwin's disappearance.

Award-winning Susan Marshall makes history in this publication. Drawing upon more than two decades of experiences as a professional author, theatre practitioner and expert educator, she introduces a theoretical discourse and a practical framework for a new theatrical style for the stage. In her groundbreaking article: *Theatre Playscapes: A New Theatrical Style*, Susan examines the impacts of the twenty first century's unprecedented emphasis on individualism, within the constraints of globalisation. She argues that in our brave new world, the role of the theatre is vital in its abilities to empower our young people to choose to nurture their beings, develop autonomy and to connect with their lifeworlds.

In this play, *Fleur of Yesterday*, we see Susan's work with the Theatre Playscapes style in practise. Inspired by her travels in France, Susan has engaged in extensive research into the science of plant breeding and has created a play that speaks for the precious life of the wild flower. Drawing upon the beauty of both the English and French languages, Susan creates an evocative, energetic and mysterious play for young adults.

NOW AVAILABLE AT ALL GOOD BOOKSTORES AROUND THE GLOBE.

About the Author

Susan Marshall is a novelist, fiction writer, poet, dramatist and essayist and the founder of Story Playscapes. She is also a theatre practitioner and an expert educator. Susan is highly skilled in working with young adults in theatrical, educational and community settings and is a recipient of a prestigious award for her outstanding and extensive work with young people.

Susan's love for the arts began in early childhood. She discovered she had a strong physical connection with her surroundings (her playscapes) and could work with moments of energetic motions, letting them breathe and take flight through writing and performance work. She has fond memories of her parents encouraging her to read and write stories. She would also decorate her backyard with sheets as curtains and invite her parents as audience members to share in her performance work.

Susan's first productions were in primary school, under the experienced guidance of her significant teachers: Kim Young and Stu Cooper. She portrayed the Narrator in the stage adaptation of Road Dahl's *James and the Giant Peach*. In her French studies, she also had the fortune to portray the King in the French stage adaptation of *Le Petit Prince* by Antoine de Saint-Exupéry.

In secondary school, Susan felt blessed to be taught English and Drama by Di Gagen, the professional Australian theatre critic and stage director. Di was instrumental in helping Susan to discover and harness her artistic nature and skills. Under Di's guidance, Susan learnt how to critique live theatrical performance and to further develop and refine her writing skills.

Di Gagen also trained Susan in the art of theatre direction, by allowing her to take on the role of Stage Director for the productions: *Just Equal* by Dennis Betts and *A Midsummer Night's Dream* by William Shakespeare. Susan also had the privilege of being taught the skills of professional pantomimic performance when she was cast as various roles, including Phoebe and a Field Mouse in A. A. Milne's *Toad of Toad Hall*, which was co-directed by Di and Steve Gagen at the Hartwell Players in Melbourne.

Di Gagen also introduced Susan to the world of St Martin's Youth Arts Centre in Melbourne. Susan spent many years there, further developing her skills in performance. She was privileged to be trained in the techniques of improvisation by the experienced Geoff Wallis and even participated in a number of *Theatresports* regional finals.

Another highlight for Susan at St Martin's Youth Arts Centre, was the opportunity to be trained by the professional actor, James Wardlaw, in Stanislavski's method acting techniques. Susan also worked closely with the highly esteemed Artistic Director, Brett Adam, on devising and writing the script for the production of *Orb.IT* for the Melbourne International Arts Festival. As an actor, Susan also enjoyed portraying various roles in the non-realistic production within the modern set design created by Darryl Cordell.

Susan attended La Trobe University, where she completed a Bachelor of Arts and majored in English and Theatre and Drama. In her English degree, she committed herself to learning to read, analyse and write a range of narrative types, from classical to post structuralist. Professor Richard Freadman was a significant lecturer for Susan, due to his encouragement of her reading and analysis skills in autobiographical texts; along with broadening her understandings of the notions of the self in writing and literary theory.

In her Theatre and Drama degree, Susan was fortunate to be taught the art of theatre performance and theory by the highly experienced and esteemed, late Geoffrey Milne. She was also blessed to learn from the amazing expertise of the theatre practitioners: Julian Meyrick, Peta Tait and Meredith Rogers.

At La Trobe University, Susan also enjoyed portraying various roles in the theatrical production: *As You Like It*, by William Shakespeare, directed by Meredith Rogers and performed at the Trades Hall in Melbourne. She also performed the protagonist in the post structuralist production of Virginia Baxter's *What Time is This House?* at the Melbourne Fringe Festival. Later, she performed Phrygenia in the production *Spartacus and Phrygenia*, (written and directed by Peter and Corinne at Créations Barquette Gitane), for the Banyule Festival in Melbourne.

Keen to learn more about theatre direction, Susan had the privilege of observing and being taught by the professional stage director, Richard Keown, as he directed the Australian premiere production of John Harrison's *Holidays* at Peridot Theatre in Melbourne. Later, Susan had the privilege of directing the Australian premiere production of Timothy Daly's *Beach: A Theatrical Fantasia* with a young cast.

Always passionate about the arts and wanting to share her knowledge with young people, Susan completed a postgraduate Bachelor of Education: Primary and Secondary, at Deakin University and was privileged to learn from the expertise of her amazing lecturers: Dr Jo O'Mara and Dr Jo Raphael.

Susan has taught professionally in primary and secondary schools for more than a decade and has undertaken the role of Head of Drama. Susan has also written a number of drama and literacy articles for academic publications and mentored pre-service and practising teachers. She has presented at state and national conferences in drama and literacy education, including at the Victorian College of the Arts, the University of Melbourne and at the Queensland University of Technology in Brisbane and has also worked as an executive committee member for Drama Victoria.

As time progressed, Susan immersed herself in the adventures of play writing with the intention of developing works for young adults to explore in the classroom or youth theatre settings. This led to the development of her play: *Broken World*, which was published by RMDesigned in 2013. The play was launched at the joint AATE/ALEA National Conference and positively reviewed by the Children's Book Council of Australia. RMDesigned also published Susan's second play, *Indigo's Haven* in 2016.

Susan has also written a range of publications, which have been published at Vocal Media in the U.S.A. These include, Susan's poems: *Grandpa Ben's Mysterious Notebook: A Tale*; *A Day Spent: the Playful Thoughts of a Tired Mind*; *My Nature Spirit: A Poem Celebrating my Connection with Nature*; *Is Summer Still Aglow Within Thy Heart?: The Eternal Shore of Summer Love*; *Winter's Breath: Mother Nature's Precious Time* and *Heart's Land*, along with her short stories: *Paper Jilu: A Journey of Her Notes*; *Gail's Red Horizon: A Fantastical Adventure*; *Hidden Magic: Part 1*; *Peonies for Masha: Her Journey Home* (shortlisted as a finalist in the Vocal+ Fiction Awards, 2022); *Stay* and *Tace's Lost Spirit: Searching for Vie*.

Susan is an honoured recipient of the prestigious *Award for Special Civic Service*, which was presented to her by the Mayor of Richmond, Victoria, for her extensive civic contributions to the city of Richmond and the Richmond City Council. The Award particularly recognises her outstanding efforts in assisting young people through her work on the Richmond Youth Work Project and the Richmond Youth Council.

In 2020, Susan founded Story Playscapes, her writing and publishing business. It was here that she became globally renown for delving into her playscapes when developing her writing. Susan's written works are highly respected by a dedicated global audience.

As an author, theatre practitioner and educator, Susan brings a wealth of knowledge to Story Playscapes. She is passionate about empowering literacy development in her global readership. Susan is also big hearted in her discussions on social media, where she fosters a love for reading and discovery in her readers.

In 2022, Susan was privileged to collaborate with the world class designer, Ryan Marshall, on the book design of her debut novel: *Makeshift Girl: The Secret Heritage Trail*. A literary fiction, it is book one of the Makeshift Girl series and is also Susan's debut novel for adults. The Hardcover Collector's Edition also includes the publication of her Romantic poem: *Evergold Dream*. In 2023, the novel was released to book retailers and readers around the globe.

In 2023, Susan continued her collaboration with Ryan Marshall and was honoured that he designed her play publication for young adults: *Fleur of Yesterday*. It is the first play released in Story Playscapes' new Theatre Playscapes series. In the publication, Susan was also proud to officially present her monumental achievement: her new Theatre Playscapes theatrical style, developed for young performers, to readers and theatre makers around the world.

Susan is delighted to release *All the Hope We Carry*, the second play for young adults in her new Theatre Playscapes series. The publication is also designed by Ryan Marshall. Susan has used her exceptional ability to distil and transcend vivid, dream-like moments, which evoke the spirit of the war survivor on a compelling and fantastical journey of hope.

Acknowledgements

In creating this book, I continue to acknowledge the wonderful presence and growth of young people in our world. In presenting *All the Hope we Carry*, I aim to provide our young people with opportunities to engage with their own special, unique presence through life and theatre.

I acknowledge the special connection I had with my late Nanna, who I was privileged to know and love. It is her story that inspired my creation of this play.

I wish to thank the amazing, global readership of Story Playscapes. To be able to share my work with you is a privilege that I will always be grateful for.

A special thank you to Ryan Marshall, my collaborator, who continues to amaze me with his extraordinary skills in photography, digital art and design work for this book.

About the Book Designer

Ryan Marshall is a graphic designer, photographer and illustrator, with more than 20 years of experience in designing a broad range of monographs, trade and fiction publications for world-leading professionals in the arts, design, photographic, automotive, landscape design and architectural industries.

Ryan has applied his unique technical skill set to the design and creation of hundreds of titles and includes significant contributions to international bestselling publications and series.

In 2022, Ryan collaborated with Susan Marshall and designed Story Playscapes' publications: *Makeshift Girl: The Secret Heritage Trail* and *Fleur of Yesterday*. Both publications are currently available at book retailers around the globe.

Ryan is delighted to continue to collaborate with Susan Marshall and bring his highly proficient design and technical expertise to the book design, photography and digital art for her play: *All the Hope We Carry*.

It is a rewarding experience for Ryan to collaborate with Susan and to bring her wonderful stories to the printed page for readers to discover and enjoy!

About Story Playscapes

Story Playscapes, established in 2020, is an Australian writing and publishing business founded by Australian Author, Susan Marshall.

The business is dedicated to promoting positive approaches to literacy development. It nurtures a global readership by actively sharing Susan Marshall's diverse range of written works on its website and via print and ebook publications.

In 2023, Story Playscapes released its premiere publication: *Makeshift Girl: The Secret Heritage Trail* by Susan Marshall. It is book one of the Makeshift Girl series and is also Susan's debut novel for adults. In the same year, Story Playscapes also released *Fleur of Yesterday,* the first play written by Susan Marshall in her exciting new Theatre Playscapes series for young adults. The monumental publication also revealed her new Theatre Playscapes style. Both publications are currently available at book retailers around the globe.

Story Playscapes is honoured to release *All the Hope We Carry* by Susan Marshall. It is the second play in her new Theatre Playscapes series. Susan has used her exceptional ability to distil and transcend vivid, dream-like moments, which evoke the spirit of the war survivor on a compelling and fantastical journey of hope.

Story Playscapes

DISCOVER THE STORY

🌐 www.storyplayscapes.com

f Facebook: /storyplayscapes

⊙ Instagram: @storyplayscapes

www.ingramcontent.com/pod-product-compliance
Lightning Source LLC
Chambersburg PA
CBHW070341120726
47909CB00008B/2710